My One True Love

STEPHANIE TAYLOR

Clean Reads
www.cleanreads.com

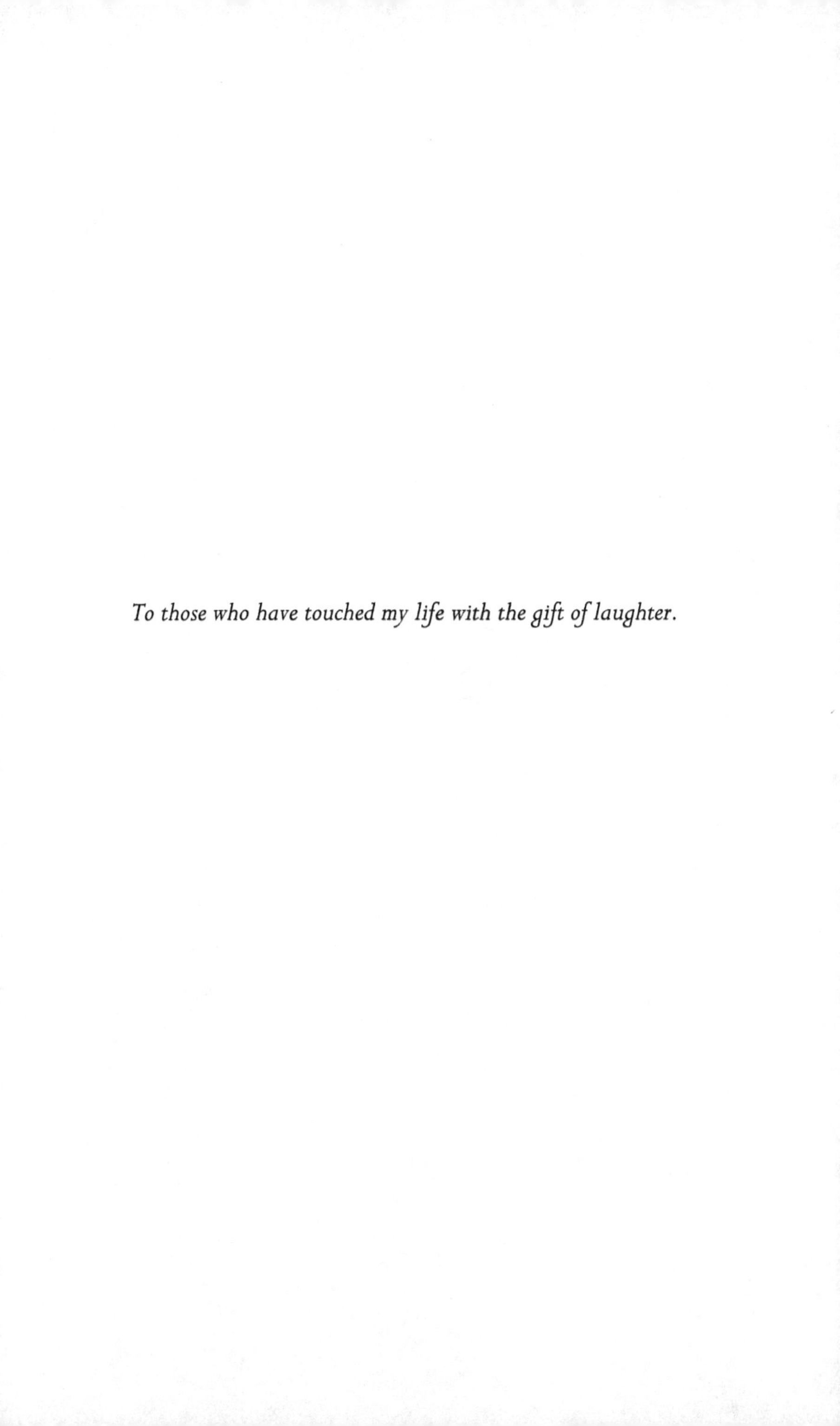

To those who have touched my life with the gift of laughter.

Chapter 1

Jason Kenyon was poised with his axe to chop a tree for fire-wood at the base of the mountain behind his cabin. The ground beneath him started to tremble. A gunshot reverberated off the mountains and then a freight train-like sound immediately alerted his senses. He smelled the sharp, cold odor of snow. Lots of snow.

Despite the near complete sunset, he could still see the white mass above him at the top of the mountain, moving. Quickly looking around, he found a tree old and thick enough to withstand his weight and the avalanche. He used his axe as a handle to help him climb it. With great heaves and sweat breaking out on his forehead, he made it to the midway point and held on to the trunk for dear life. The avalanche rumbled past him, and the tree underneath his arms vibrated and creaked. His heart pounded, not only from the climb, but from fear.

Even though he was a trained park ranger for the small town of Oakley, he hadn't been in this situation before. There was certainly enough snow to justify one, but in his memory, the area had never suffered from an avalanche.

Jason watched the snow mound higher and higher against the tree, and he found himself praying silently. As the avalanche slowed, the blanket of white was suddenly interrupted by a patch of dark blue and red. Without thinking twice, he jumped into the waist deep snow, his legs aching with the effort it took to move forward. Shards of ice tore at his jeans and his shin grazed something sharp.

Gritting his teeth, he pushed through the pain and snow until he finally grasped the small hand, one that had to belong to a woman.

He was ashamed his first thought had been about his own safety and not a hiker or skier caught up in the snow. But his second thought reminded him he still had a job to do, and getting this woman to safety was his first priority. Since he was close enough to his cabin, he'd take her there and radio in to the sheriff that she'd been found.

He tugged on the hand, which he noticed had red fingernails, and huffed when she didn't budge. Kneeling as much as he could, he burrowed a path underneath her shoulders with his gloved hands and placed his arms around her middle. Using all of his strength, he pulled. He let out a sigh of relief when the limp body came up out of the icy snow. Brushing away the snow from her neck, he checked her vitals and found a strong pulse, thankful he found one at all. He had never seen a dead body outside of a funeral home and never wanted to.

Jason didn't take the time to brush all the dark curls away from her face to see if he might know her. Oakley was a small town, after all. But getting her warmed up was his main concern. He'd work on identification later. Without another thought, he bent, scooped her up into his arms, and headed for his cabin.

So much for getting that firewood he wanted.

⚬

I'm so cold.

Liz Henley burrowed against Patrick's heated body as a shiver slid down her spine. "Put your arms around me," she whispered, wincing as sharp blades of pain scraped her throat.

"You'll be fine, Lizzie. Just rest."

Something inside of Liz grew even colder. That deep, smooth timbre, so unlike Patrick's businesslike tone, definitely didn't belong to her fiancé. It was the voice of a million dreams that had haunted her for seven years. Lizzie. Even though she knew he wasn't real, she snuggled closer to his heat, reveling in the thrill of her dream. Oh, how she'd missed Jason. Missed him so much, it was now a physical ache. But she was definitely dreaming. No way would Jason be holding her in his arms like this. Not after what she did to him.

Another shudder wracked her body, and she pulled his arms around her. Since this was her fantasy, she could allow herself to be taken away by the comforting feel of his embrace and the yearning of her body. She tried to open her eyes to see his handsome face, but they wouldn't cooperate. Of course not, it was a dream.

Before she slipped back into unconsciousness, she said the words she'd wanted to say for so long. Maybe they would give her a measure of peace when her wedding day arrived. "I still love you, Jason."

She felt his grip on her tighten. "Rest," he whispered, and his lips brushed tenderly against hers.

And she did.

Chapter 2

Liz dreamed she was in a different place. It was cold. For some reason, she heard the rolling thunder of logs being dumped into a wood stove, and the clank of the top lid.

She rolled, tossing off the quilt; it felt sticky and heavy against her sweaty skin. Why would Patrick be using a wood stove? She heard a door open and shut. A blast of frigid air made the sweat on her skin sting. She reached for the discarded quilt, tunneling under it, trying to go back to the quiet peace of her dreams, where her head no longer pounded from such a little fall, and Jason held her snug in his arms. But she couldn't. She was awake, and she wasn't dreaming anymore.

Her eyes opened and she saw she was inside a log cabin. The décor was sparse with a few pictures hanging on the walls; the quilt on the bed matched the sheets. A small dresser sat in the corner next to a door she assumed was a closet.

As she registered her surroundings, a big lumberjack strolled into her room, dressed in a flannel shirt and worn jeans. A thick beard covered everything but his eyes, nose, and forehead.

Panic turned her blood icy, and by the time she thought to pretend sleep, he'd noticed she was awake. His blue eyes crinkled as he smiled underneath all the fuzz.

"Good morning," he greeted and walked over to her.

He was huge. His arms bulged under sleeves rolled up to his elbows. Jeans hugged his thighs as he sat down on the edge of the bed. It dipped under his weight. Liz wasn't sure what to do with this stranger. There was only one man she'd ever known that big in size. Her eyebrows furrowed.

"How are you feeling?" he asked softly.

She studied the man. His voice was kind and so familiar. Her dreams came back to her, and she wondered if it could be...

"Who are you?" she croaked. Tugging at the sheets, she pulled them up to her chin. She felt naked even though she was clothed in flannel pajamas five sizes too big.

Wait, she hadn't been wearing pajamas, especially ones this big. She touched the neck of the oversized pajamas and looked at the man. His knowing smirk meant only one thing. He'd changed her clothes!

"Where am I?" she demanded, forcing strength into her quivering voice.

"You're in my cabin at the base of the mountain. You fell and I just happened to be there when you went sailing by."

A lump formed in her throat. The more he spoke, the more memories hit her. The warmth, the dreams of being held skin to skin in a safe haven, was it all a dream, or was it reality? She cringed. This man couldn't be Jason.

"Who are you?"

His eyes crinkled again. "You don't know?"

"Would I ask if I knew?" But, dear heavens, she feared she did know.

His full lips pulled upward, but served to do nothing more than move a few hairs of his thick, brown beard. "Good point. I think you remember me as Jason Kenyon. Your ex-fiancé."

Liz's eyes stung with unshed tears. It had been years since she looked into those eyes or been the subject of his smile. He had a beautiful smile when he wasn't so furry.

"Lizzie." he whispered when he saw her tears, and stretched out his hand to touch her face.

Appalled she had shown weakness, she flinched away. Then a new thought hit her. Her wedding! "Oh no! What day is it?"

"February twelfth, why?"

"I've got to get back into town! I'm getting married in two days." She struggled against the pain pulsing through her head and pushed at the covers to stand up.

Jason's gentle, giant hands pushed her shoulders back against the headboard. His fingertips played with the ends of her hair before he smoothed it behind her ear. "We can't get back to town."

Horror filled her. "Why not?"

"The roads are impassable. Until the snow plows come through after Valentine's Day, we're stuck."

"You've got to be kidding."

"Do I look like I'm kidding?"

She looked at him but found the dark beard so distracting, her annoyance level rose. "You don't look like anything but a hairy lumberjack. When was the last time you shaved?"

Jason rolled his eyes. "You never did care for facial hair."

Liz focused on her anger and shot him a glare. The last thing she wanted was to remember their past together. She'd gone up to the mountain to think her wedding through and put the past behind her. That was the last thing she remembered. Unfortunately, she couldn't remember if she'd come to a conclusion or not.

With a loud exhale, Jason stood and paced the room. "Getting married, huh?" he asked and ran his fingers through his wavy, dark hair. "Does he know you're prone to running?"

"Shut up." She'd always hated this about him, the smugness, the conceit. It was like he knew everything about her. Liz had news for him, she wasn't the same girl he knew from high school!

His hands rose in defense as he sighed. "Just asking a question. I figure any man stupid enough to get involved with you gets what's coming to him."

Liz stood up and ignored the dizziness as it swamped her.

"What's that supposed to mean?"

"Exactly what I said, sweetheart. He's stupid."

Liz felt like a child as she stamped her foot, but she couldn't think of anything else to do when she stood so close to his masculine smell, like pine needles and coffee.

"He's a doctor. He's not stupid."

"Books smarts don't equal common sense, honey."

With narrowed eyes, she debated on whether to shove him or slap him. The predatory gleam in his eye told her both would earn some serious consequences, so she chose to do neither.

"You're still hot for me," he said with a knowing grin.

She flashed her diamond in his direction. "Does this look like I'm still hot for you, Kenyon? Who would have the hots for a man who looks like Paul Bunyan?"

"You."

"Know what I've always hated about you?"

"That I'm always right?"

The tint of the room took on a red hue. He was always able to provoke this kind of reaction from her, and she refused to let him know he still did.

"Jason, I'm getting married in two days and I can promise you, I haven't thought of you once in the seven years since I left you." Seven years, eight months, three weeks and two days, to be exact.

Jason's blue eyes cooled. "I should have left you in the snow." Liz gave him a sweet smile.

"But you didn't."

"To my everlasting shame," he said, with an equally saccharine smile.

Letting out a frustrated sigh, she sat on the edge of the bed, mainly to deflect the dizziness.

"Do you feel okay? You look like you're about to pass out." He came around the end of the bed to stand in front of her. "Are you hungry?"

Liz debated whether or not to tell him the truth. She didn't want to owe him anything, but the truth was she could gnaw her own arm off. "Yes," she muttered.

"I'll bring you some food."

The last thing she wanted was Jason serving her food in bed. "I can walk."

His skeptical gaze upped her annoyance level. "Can you make it to the kitchen?"

"Of course I can."

He tucked his hand gently underneath her arm and helped her stand. The dizziness caused her to sway, but she refused to lean into Jason. A whimper escaped her lips, and she grabbed the footboard of the bed to steady herself.

"You're the most stubborn woman I've ever met," he growled.

The next thing she knew, her world tilted. This time, Jason carried her.

"Put me down!" Liz cried at the sudden closeness.

"Stop wiggling like that, or I'll put you down right where I'm standing. I would love to watch you land on your sweet behind."

Afraid he meant what he said, she stopped moving. Her whole body ached from the fall, and she was pretty sure she couldn't withstand any more bruises. "I hate you."

"No, you don't."

The smug tone of his words served to further infuriate her, but she didn't say anything as he moved out of the bedroom and into the small kitchen area. He plopped her down in a chair.

"What'll it be? Chicken noodle soup, chicken noodle soup, or chicken noodle soup?"

Liz glared.

"So, I have to know why you came back to Oakley to get married. I thought this place was too backwoods for you. You needed to feel free."

She grimaced at his mockery of their last conversation. "I always loved the town, but not the people."

He grunted. "Surely good ole Neva didn't run you off. I know she's annoying, but that's just giving her too much power. So, what scared you the most, Lizzie? Being stuck here or being my wife?"

"Don't," Liz warned. A stab of longing hit her square in the gut. Some days she felt like leaving was the best thing she'd ever done, but most days? She regretted not becoming his wife, waking up next to him every morning, making love whenever the mood struck. They'd been so good together before she got spooked and high--tailed it out of Oakley.

"Oh, I think it's about seven years too late myself, but that doesn't mean I don't want to hear what you have to say."

"You know why I left you. Everything else is none of your business."

He gave a careless shrug as he opened a can of soup. "Suit yourself."

How did one man possess the ability to rile her so much? What was it about him that made her want to scream?

But she knew the answer. She'd known it for seven years now. She'd never gotten over Jason Kenyon. Even with a ring on her finger and a wedding to another man scheduled to happen in two days, she realized she still loved him. Sure, she'd tried to put her love for Jason behind her as best she could, but it obviously hadn't been enough. She buried her face in her hands.

Of all the people to rescue her, why did it have to be the very person she'd gone to the mountain to put behind her? She would have been completely happy to go ahead and marry Patrick if Jason hadn't continued popping up in her mind. Even if she didn't love Patrick with the same intensity she'd once had for Jason, he was a good man and could provide her and any children they had with a stable home and a decent life. That wasn't a bad thing to want, was it? But her feelings for Jason kept telling her, "yes."

At first, she'd chalked it up to being back in town. On top of that, Valentine's Day was always a little difficult because of the memories of her last one in Oakley. But putting the two together?

She let out a ragged sigh.

Jason placed a bowl under her nose. He nodded toward the soup and sat down next to her at the small table.

"I left because…"

An eyebrow raised in her direction. "Go on."

"The night before I left, we talked about our future, remember? You said you wanted to become a policeman and couldn't wait to spend the rest of our lives together."

When he raised his eyebrows, indicating he didn't follow her, she sighed again. "Here, Jason. In Oakley. I watched my mother waste away in this town. Work her fingers to the bone at a stupid glove mill because it was the only option she had here. I didn't want to resent you. You were happy staying here, and I wasn't. I wanted more than a career in slave labor and two point five kids. Things would have been different if we had wanted the same things."

"So you thought leaving in the middle of the night and not saying goodbye would make it easier?"

"No, but I was only eighteen. I didn't know what to do."

He shoved a spoonful of soup in his mouth and waited until he swallowed to speak. "Well, I can tell you right now, running didn't help matters. I think if you had stuck around long enough to talk to me about this, we could have worked something out."

"Maybe not. It was a long time ago. And I'm marrying someone else now."

"I told you. You're stuck here until the plows come through next week. I've already radioed in to Sheriff Bagley to let everyone know that you're with me."

Liz sat up straight, mouth agape. "You did what?"

"I didn't stutter."

"Your sister is going to have her boyfriend put this all over the newspaper, Jason. Patrick's going to think I came here on purpose!" He gave another one of his not-my-fault shrugs.

"I asked you if you warned him about your track record. I can't help what people think. And why were you so stupid to go to the mountain alone in the middle of winter without tracking equipment, anyway? You're lucky I happened to be in the right place at the right time."

"It's debatable," she shot at him.

"Let's put it this way, Lizzie. If I hadn't been there to save you, you wouldn't be postponing your wedding. You'd be dead. An avalanche is serious business; you lived here long enough to know that, even if we don't see that many. You're also lucky you were near the bottom when you got caught in it."

Liz thought about that for a moment. "An avalanche? I thought I fell."

"Nope. I heard a big creaking sound and a pop and next thing I knew you came surfing by, unconscious."

The seriousness of the situation hit her full force, and a shiver ran down her spine. Liz closed her eyes to ward off his words and the reality of her brush with death. "Thank you," she said before she could reel in the words. The last thing she wanted was for him to feel like she owed him something.

"You're welcome. Now eat up."

He returned to his soup with gusto and ignored her. Liz found her appetite had left her, but she forced herself to eat some of it to get her strength back.

She had a wedding to get to.

All Jason wanted to do was grab Lizzie and hold on tight. He wanted to take away that lost little girl look and tell her everything would be all right.

Yet, the thought of repeating history made him want to run away at lightning speed. He'd been burned for his mistakes, and he wasn't about to let it happen again.

"You need to rest. You've probably got a concussion after your fall." He had to get away from her for a little while. Sitting so close, seeing the depths of her wide eyes staring at him made his heart do those funny little dances in his chest he'd sworn he never wanted to feel again.

"Yeah, I'm still pretty tired." She looked around the cabin. "Where are you going to sleep?"

"On the couch. Call if you need anything."

"Is there a TV here?"

He couldn't help but laugh. "No."

"Why not?"

"I never bothered to put one in. This place runs on a generator when the power is out. The avalanche took out all the power. And most people don't come here for TV."

"Oh." He loved how her cheeks turned a pretty pink as she caught the sexual implication.

"There are plenty of books on the shelf over there in the corner."

Liz pushed away from the table and stood. She swayed a little.

He leaped to his feet and wrapped his arms around her waist.

"You okay?" His eyes slammed shut at the feel of her soft body aligned with his. She pressed against his chest with her palms and pushed at him.

"I'm fine," she said sharply. "Let me go."

Slowly, he opened his eyes and looked at the woman he used to love. Still loved, although he didn't understand why. She'd left him without a word just when he thought his life was getting started. For seven years, he'd hung suspended in the air, waiting for her to come back or waiting for some explanation to fill the gaping hole. Oh, how he'd wanted to go after her, make her see reason. But the simple return of his engagement ring told him everything he needed to know.

Even now, she flaunted that massive rock on her finger like it was her pride and joy. But what she didn't realize yet was the happiness she continued to allude to was eluding her. Her eyes were dead.

He remembered what she'd said while she was unconscious:

I still love you, Jason.

The question was, did he believe her? He might have the moment she'd realized who he was and her eyes sparked to life, but everything from her body language to her speech screamed that she hated him.

"Let me go," she said again.

He tugged her closer.

"Don't you dare kiss me," she warned, but her hands fisted in his shirt and she leaned into him, in perfect contrast to her words.

His lips touched hers in a whispered caress. He pulled back to look at her, and he saw she wasn't angry anymore. In fact, she stared at his mouth with the same hunger he felt churning in his gut.

"We're over, Jason," she whispered.

"Far from it." He grinned, trying to convey confidence when all he felt was hesitation.

He touched his lips to hers again, giving her plenty of time to move away, but he thought she might have leaned into him a little.

Her lips felt exactly like he remembered. Her delicate and smooth touch moved over him. Sliding his fingers through her hair, careful of the bandage at her temple, he held her against him, exploring her sweetness. She responded with a sigh and relaxed. Her fingers looped behind his neck and pressed him closer.

When things started to escalate, and their breath mingled together in short, little pants, Liz pushed away from him.

"I hit my head harder than I thought," she mumbled and wiped her mouth. Then, she angled a disgusted look his way. "It's like kissing a goat."

"Maaaa," he said and walked across the small expanse of the living room, grabbing the first book he saw. He turned and lay down across the couch with his feet propped up on the end. A quick glance over his shoulder confirmed she still stood exactly where he'd left her, with her mouth hanging open.

"So, that's it?" she demanded, marching to the couch and towering over him with her hand on her hip. "You're going to kiss me and then read a book?"

"Yup." As much as it bothered him to let the woman he loved believe he didn't care, he would do what was necessary to get her back. Because he realized after her unconscious confession that she still loved him and now, with their kiss, there was no doubt in his mind. She was the one he was meant to be with. He had a little over forty-eight hours to convince the conscious Lizzie what her subconscious had already admitted to him.

"You can't do that."

"Watch me." He worked hard to keep his voice even. What he really wanted to do was to yell at her for leaving him. Or kiss her until they made up for the last seven years they'd spent apart.

Or both.

"Fine." She snatched the book closest to her off the shelf and stormed back into the bedroom.

The door slammed behind her.

It took everything Jason had not to follow her.

Chapter 3

Liz awoke and breathed in a deep, cleansing breath as she looked out the window. The sun shining through promised a beautiful day. The dizziness plaguing her since the avalanche seemed to have eased. Today, she would get back to Patrick so they could continue on with the wedding.

She didn't allow herself to think about the kiss she'd shared with Jason the night before. A mistake was a mistake. One she wouldn't let happen again.

The smell of bacon drifted to her and she sat up, cautious of the dizziness. When nothing tilted, she stood and stretched. Things weren't nearly as achy as they had been yesterday, and she was thankful. It might be a long trek in the snow if Jason refused to take her into town.

With a spring in her step, she walked out into the kitchen, and she was surprised at the feast she saw on the table.

"I thought we only had chicken noodle soup," she mused.

"For dinner, we do. But I still have a lot of stuff for breakfast. Pancakes?" he asked, poising a spatula in mid-air as he waited for her answer.

"Uh, sure." Who was she to turn down a fattening meal on the eve of her wedding?

"Take a seat, and I'll have it ready in a second. How are you feeling?"

"Good. I think I can make the walk back into town or at least to my car at the park entrance."

His confident chuckle filled her ears and made her feel like a school girl in trouble. "No, you can't."

"You can't stop me."

An eyebrow raised in a silent dare.

"You can't, Jason." There was that shrug she disliked so much.

"Maybe not, but three feet of snow might. And if the snow doesn't, the single digit temperatures will."

She glared. "Don't think you can kiss me and then boss me around."

"I haven't thought once about the kiss," he said. "You're the only one talking about it."

And then it began again, the boiling rage he could evoke so quickly, turning her from a lamb into a lion. "I haven't thought about it, either!"

"Then why did you mention it?"

"Because you're trying to keep me here on purpose like you own me or something!"

He shrugged. "If you want to walk in three feet of snow barefoot and in pajamas, be my guest."

"Where are the shoes I wore when I fell?"

"Beats me. Probably still underneath the avalanche."

"Then I'll borrow some of yours."

"Sorry honey, but the only pair I've got is on my feet. And I'm not about to sacrifice my toes in the name of your wedding."

Seething, Liz fell silent.

After a moment, a plate of piping hot breakfast slid under her nose. "Thank you," she mumbled.

While they ate in silence, Jason glanced her way a few times, but as soon as she thought he might say something, he shoveled another mouthful of food into his mouth instead.

After awhile, he said, "I've got to go out and check the mountain today by foot. Will you be all right alone?"

"Why do you have to do that?"

"It's my job."

"I thought you were a policeman."

"Nope. When Ranger Horton retired, I decided to step up and take on the job."

"Oh. Well, I'm not staying here, remember?"

"Then I guess I'll head back toward town after my rounds so I can pick your corpse out of the snow and deliver it to your waiting fiancé. At least I can take my time. The snow will preserve you nicely." As an afterthought, he added, "And I thought he was the only stupid one."

"Haha," she said.

"I'm not kidding, but if you want to find out for yourself, go right ahead. I'll radio in to Sheriff Bagley to be on the lookout."

"Jason, you know I can't stay here. My wedding is tomorrow."

Slowly standing so that he loomed over her, he glared. "Your wedding isn't important enough for either of us to risk our lives. Either you stay here, or you go on your own."

She raised her chin a notch so she could level her gaze with his. "You'd risk your life for your job, but not me. Just like a typical Oakley resident. Can I at least use the radio and see if they can get in touch with Patrick? I'd really like to explain things to him, myself."

"When I leave, go ahead. It's up in the attic next to the window. It gets better reception up there. Feel free to check my closet for an extra shirt or a sweater. There's no heat up there."

With a silent nod, she watched him don his coat, scarf, hat, and gloves and leave without a backward glance.

Jason hacked at the tree with his axe as hard as he could. His frustration level was through the roof, and he figured when he returned, he wouldn't find Lizzie waiting there for him. She was stubborn enough to head out on her own without shoes.

And if she did, well, he would let her. She didn't have to know the cabin was only a mile or so from town. She also didn't have to know about that snowmobile parked in the wood shed. If she was determined to marry the rich doctor, then who was he—a lowly park ranger—to stop her? He wouldn't deter her, but he certainly wouldn't help her.

A few days ago, his life had been nice and predictable. Now he entertained thoughts of breaking up engagements and whisking his former fiancée away from her wedding.

But he wasn't made that way. Every direction he turned it, he couldn't make himself stop her if she was determined to go through with her marriage to another man. She knew her own heart, and maybe after all these years, she really was happy. Maybe what she said was the truth: When she left him seven years ago, she hadn't looked back.

It hurt more than he wanted to admit, but wouldn't let it turn him into someone he wasn't. He'd kissed her and before things were over, he'd tell her how he felt. If that didn't change her mind, he'd pretend to get over her like he had the first time.

When the tree finally fell into the snow with a quiet swoosh, he felt like it was his heart breaking in two.

Angrily, he chopped the tree up, ignoring the bitter cold. So much for Valentine's Day and falling in love.

Even if she meant those delirious words she'd spoken during the few hours she was unconscious and she didn't love this guy, he had to trust she would recognize her feelings and do the right thing. But if she was still in the cabin, he wouldn't stop his original plan. She wouldn't marry Patrick without knowing how he felt.

Seven years was a long time to be away from someone, and when he really thought about it, he didn't know much about Lizzie anymore. She'd moved away in the middle of the night to some big city up north—Baltimore, last he'd heard—and made a life for herself without him.

Who was he to stop her now? Maybe marrying a rich doctor and living a mediocre life full of money was part of her plan.

But one old cliche remained true: Money couldn't buy happiness.

⤜⧽

He'd been gone several hours and didn't expect to find her sitting at the small kitchen table with a crossword puzzle when he returned.

His heart sped up at the sight of her brown eyes zeroing in on him when he walked through the door and shook off his boots.

"What's a five letter word for high-maintenance?" she asked, tapping the pen against her chin.

"Women," he mumbled.

She shot him a look of annoyance but didn't say anything. "Did you decide missing a few toes wouldn't accessorize your wedding dress the way you wanted?"

"I radioed in and Sheriff Bagley was able to get Patrick on the line. He's going to try to rent a snowmobile to come out here and pick me up." She paused. "We're still getting married," she added softly. To Jason, it sounded like an apology.

Fed up with himself and the crazy rollercoaster of emotions, he turned his back to her as he removed his winter gear. He couldn't look at her right now.

The chair she sat in creaked, and her soft footsteps padded across the room. She stood behind him, but he couldn't turn to look at her. Not with the huge lump in his throat.

"Jason." She laid a soft hand on his shoulder and the note of sympathy in her voice cracked his carefully controlled façade.

He whirled around to face her. "What do you want me to say? Congratulations? Or how about I think you're making the biggest mistake of your life, besides running out on me to begin with? Would it change anything?"

She smiled sadly. "No."

Those brown eyes penetrated his. He could see she wanted to believe herself by the stubborn tilt of her chin, but those eyes told a different story.

His control broke. The anger washed away, and sorrow filled its place. "What if I told you I wish things had been different for us? That maybe somehow I knew you would run, and I came after you and stopped you? Would that change anything?"

"We wanted different things, Jason. We still do. Marrying Patrick is the right thing for me to do. He understands me."

But he understood her better. He'd practically grown up with her. "Do you love him?"

Her gaze left his for a moment. "I love him enough."

"Why would you ever settle for anything less than what you deserve? Has city life jaded you so much?"

"Patrick and I have a lot in common. We love to read, discuss our jobs, take a morning run together. We both want to be married."

"Sounds like a match made in heaven." Jason reached out to take her hand and pull her into his arms. "Tell me you don't think about me."

"I don't think about you." She swallowed then licked her lips as her eyes riveted to his mouth.

"Tell me you really want to marry Patrick."

"I want to marry Patrick."

"Tell me you don't want to kiss me right now." Before he thought twice, he swooped down, intent on showing her exactly what she was missing with good ole Patrick. But his lips met her cheek as she turned her head at the last second.

"I don't kiss goats."

Jason wasn't sure if he wanted to laugh until he cried or just cry. Maybe a little of both. How much longer would he torture himself?

For years now, he'd thought only of her smile, the way she challenged him when no one else could. How her brown eyes turned to melted chocolate when he held her. And he thought of that night she'd agreed to become his wife. The future he wanted to share with her was right in front of him, complete with a picket fence, minivan, and two point five children. But the night she left, his dreams had gone with her. He'd felt like only an empty shell since she'd been gone.

Clearing his throat, he released her and stepped away. "I got wood on the porch out there. I thought with it being close to Valentine's Day and all, we could sit by the fire and enjoy some memories."

She gave him a cautious smile as her eyes flew to the door. "Do you have hot chocolate?"

"Yup. I'll bring the firewood in if you'll get it started. Second cabinet on the right." Without waiting for her to say another word, he walked outside without the protection of his gloves or hat. The cold seeped into his bones and reminded him that being numb was better than feeling.

In less than a single day, the woman he'd always loved would belong to someone else. Jason wasn't sure what to do anymore.

Chapter 4

"I found some." The words died on Liz's lips as she came down the attic steps and Jason was nowhere in sight.

With a heave, she placed the cold box from the attic on the couch and opened it up. The smell of dust and old cardboard met her nose. Liz pulled the string of clear Christmas lights out. It would be pretty to have them on the mantle. Valentine's Day was a hopeful holiday; she'd always loved to use it as an excuse to bring some color into a dull, gray wintery world. She wasn't doing anything romantic for her and Jason. No, of course not. Decorating the cabin was strictly for her benefit.

"You remember the last time we did this?" Jason's rumbling voice sounded behind her.

Liz didn't look up. Instead, she remembered eight Valentine's Days ago when Jason gave her an engagement ring. Inside a perfect, red rose was the small diamond she knew he'd worked all summer for the year before. That night had been magical for them both.

Swallowing past the lump in her throat, she turned to look at him. Her breath hitched at the sight before her.

He'd showered and shaved. He looked like the man who'd given her that ring. The man she'd loved. And still loved, even though she didn't want to. He leaned against the doorframe with a confidence most men could only dream about. His full lips tilted upward at her look of shock.

He held his hands out to present himself. "I decided that I didn't like being referred to as a goat."

Liz gave him a small smile as she tried to take a few deep breaths and coax her heart into a slower rhythm. Time had only made him more handsome. Laugh lines around his eyes crinkled at her when she still didn't speak. She could smell the humid, piney aftershave he'd put on, emanating from the steamy bathroom.

"Is it that bad, Lizzie?" he asked.

"You haven't changed at all."

"You used to tell me I was pretty hot, so I'm going to say that's a good thing."

"Yeah," she whispered.

With one foot, he pushed away from the doorframe and walked over to her. His scent preceded him, and she closed her eyes and inhaled. Nothing about him had changed. That same woodsy smell he'd branded all his own still had the power to make her knees go weak. The dimple she'd always loved flashed at her from the corner of his lip.

"I see you went looking for lights. Like the night I proposed."

"Mmm," Liz muttered. She hadn't been doing it intentionally, but he was right. Her subconscious automatically linked Valentine's Day with white, sparkling lights, covered with little red plastic hearts like he'd covered the gazebo in when he'd asked her to marry him. Her eyes opened. He stood directly in front of her but didn't touch her as he reached past her into the box. Somewhere during the last few minutes, she'd dropped them.

"These look familiar," Jason mused and lifted the string of lights to inspect them. "Judging the fact you're white as a sheet tells me they look familiar to you, too."

"I...I think I've seen them before, somewhere."

Jason nodded. "I still have it, you know."

"What?" Liz's breath hitched; she was intrigued yet terrified to hear what "it" was.

"Your ring. Your mom gave it back to me after she found it in your bedroom. I wanted to pawn it, but sometimes, I still look at it to remind myself of better times."

"Why haven't you married, Jason?" It was a stupid question, but she had to know. An unseen force in her soul pushed the words out of her mouth as if she had no control over her own body.

He fiddled with the lights in a nervous gesture then shrugged. "I haven't fallen in love with anyone else."

Liz realized all over again the pain he must have gone through. She'd never fully allowed herself to think about the consequences of her actions, but now, as he stood before her with a sadness she'd never seen before haunting his eyes, she knew it had been much harder on him than she ever imagined. Somewhere along the way she'd convinced herself Oakley was what he wanted. Now she wasn't so sure.

"I'm sorry, Jason," she said in a voice barely above a whisper.

He bit his lower lip and looked away. "I don't think about it much."

She smiled. If he thought about it half as much as she did, he was just as consumed with it as she was. "Liar."

Jason grinned. "Yeah, I am."

"I really am sorry. I was selfish and went on with my life. I thought you would rather stay here than be with me."

"You make me sound like a martyr."

"No. I mean, I dealt with it in my own way, but when I left, it was what I wanted. If I had thought you'd come with me, we might be down a different road now."

"But we're not." "Nope."

"And you're getting married tomorrow."

"Yes."

He wrenched away from her, tossing the lights back into the box. He walked into the kitchen. "Did you make the hot cocoa?"

She hesitated at the change of subject. "Yes."

He busied himself pouring the hot chocolate. Her heart ached to go to him and make things right. When she was honest with herself, she knew Jason was the one to rescue her for a reason. She couldn't get married until she resolved her feelings for him.

And she wasn't married yet. Tonight, she would make sure there were no doubts left in her mind about Jason. When she walked down the aisle to Patrick, she wanted only to see the face of the man she was about to marry, not the face of the one she wished she had.

⌒

Jason's hands shook a little as he handed Lizzie the mug of hot cocoa.

"The lights look good on the mantle." He gestured with his chin and sat next to her. She wrapped her fingers around the mug. Her innocent brown eyes met his briefly when their fingers touched.

"No thanks to you." She smiled at him over the rim of the cup as she took a delicate sip. She squinted when the hot liquid met her lips.

He'd turned on the radio in the kitchen to a music station right outside of town. The soft words of a ballad lilted through the air. The fire he'd built after bringing the firewood in still burned and crackled. The white strand of lights and the fire were the only illumination in the cabin. Shadows fell across Lizzie's face.

"This is nice," she said at the end of a sigh. "I haven't had a quiet evening like this in years."

Uh uh. He didn't want to hear about what she did at night. "How's your head?"

"Fine. The cut scabbed over. But I think I'll have a nice war scar to remember this Valentine's Day by."

A war scar, indeed. Like the one on his heart. They were a matched set.

He couldn't help it. He reached out and touched her hair, allowing the silkiness of it to fall through his fingers. "You'll always be beautiful to me," he rasped.

Lizzie's whole body went still; she paused with the mug half way to her lips. After what seemed like an eternity, she placed it on the coffee table and turned to Jason. She took his cup and did the same with it.

Hesitantly, she scooted over to him. Before he knew what she intended, she wrapped her arms around his waist, and she burrowed her head into his neck. Pulling her close, he placed a kiss on the top of her head. He mourned all of the years they could have done this very thing: Enjoy each other's company.

"What are we doing, Lizzie?" he asked.

"From my viewpoint, I'd say we're snuggling. You?"

"I don't know, but it feels nice."

"Like I was never gone, huh?" she murmured.

But the span of time had still separated them, and come tomorrow his misery would start all over again. So was it wrong to stop thinking about tomorrow and enjoy the moment? He'd lived for years on the memories they'd made before she left. He might make it another seven if they could make a few new ones tonight.

Lizzie's warm breath on his skin stirred awareness throughout his body. Every exhale caused the hairs on his neck to stand up. Her hand came away from his waist, and her palm rested on the side of his neck. It took him a moment to register the feeling of her lips working against his throat and the soft sighs he remembered all too well.

"Lizzie," he protested, although he wasn't sure if he wanted her to continue or stop.

In one motion, Liz pulled herself up, straddled his waist, and gave him a kiss he wasn't likely to forget any time soon.

The passion in her, as her tongue wasted no time delving deep, caused his fingers to clench on her hips and pull her against him roughly. But after a few moments, he wasn't sure which of them was the aggressor when their breath mingled and their hands were everywhere.

Jason filled his palm with her soft body, wishing the clothing they wore didn't separate them. But in a way, he was glad it did because he wouldn't have been able to think things through otherwise.

He speared his fingers through her curls and held her face against his as he tried to bring back some semblance of control. She attempted to ignore him, but he moved away from her mouth and trailed kisses down her neck and jaw.

As he pulled away from her, he touched his forehead against hers. He drew in several deep breaths to calm his libido and summon his courage.

He moved her to sit on the sofa next to him. He couldn't think clearly with her lithe body so close. But still, he couldn't stop touching her. He took her hand and joined their fingers, unwilling to let the moment pass.

He'd vowed the second she'd said in her sleep she didn't love Patrick to tell her he still cared. It looked like it was now or never.

Squaring his shoulders, he took a deep breath and said, "I still love you."

Tears sprang into Liz's eyes, and her bottom lip quivered. For a long while, she simply studied their hands together, traced her finger up and down his wrist. Her tears fell in silence. But when she looked at him again, his heart leapt.

"I still love you, too, Jason. I don't think I ever stopped."

"Don't marry him, Lizzie. If you're not sure about canceling it, at least give it another few months until we work this out."

She shook her head with a frown. "I know you're right, but it's not so simple. There are still so many things I'm not sure can ever be resolved." She shook her head and smiled through tears. "But you're right. I can't marry Patrick feeling this way."

"No?" Air filled his lungs and went out in a huge whoosh, and he forgot to inhale. He pulled her into his arms and squeezed. Dizziness assailed him before he remembered to breathe again.

"No," she confirmed.

When they pulled apart, joy sluiced through him like a gigantic, tingling wave. He couldn't wipe the smile from his face, but then again, he didn't want to.

"Can you forgive me for everything that happened, Jason? For leaving you?"

Tenderly, he trailed his finger along her jaw and smiled.

"Done."

"What now? Do we start over?"

Swallowing past the lump in his throat, Jason gave her a real smile, his heart full of love. He kissed her and reveled in the reality they were finally in each other's arms again.

"Yes," he said against her lips. "Let's start with a toast. Our hot chocolate is getting cold."

"You know that legend about the falling star you told me when you asked me to marry you?" Liz asked Jason as they sipped from their mugs in the dim light.

He remembered the legend he'd heard all of his life. Make a wish on a falling star on Valentine's Day about your one true love, and it'll come true.

"Yeah."

"I saw one while I was up on the mountain, before the avalanche. It wasn't dark yet, but it caught my attention, streaking through the sky. I made a wish and my wish came true."

Jason's hand went still mid-air as his gaze locked with hers.

Finally, his hand dropped with a loud thwack against his thigh.

"Really. What wish was that?"

He watched Liz's brows came together in a frown. "To see you again before I got married."

Jason rubbed his chin thoughtfully. "Is that why you were up on the mountain? You always did want to be alone when you needed to think."

Liz remembered back to the evening of the avalanche. She had gone to the mountain to evaluate her future and put Jason behind her for good. Little did she know fate had something else in store.

"Yeah. I thought I could just decide to be over you. I should have known better."

Jason remained quiet for a long time. Then he asked, "What are you going to do now, Lizzie?"

"I guess I'll call Patrick and let him know. Knowing this isn't over between us changes things."

"So you won't marry him?"

Liz shrugged. "I can't."

Jason let out a breath, and it fanned her hair. "Lizzie, you've made me a happy man."

She smiled. "Glad to be of service."

With a chuckle, Jason pulled her into his arms and kissed her softly. It was as if time had suddenly vanished, and they were eighteen again. Liz felt lighter than she had in years.

"I love you, Lizzie."

"I love you, too."

As he kissed her, he walked her backward toward the bedroom.

But Liz pulled away and gave him a pleading glance as she placed her hands on his shoulders. "I can't. Not until I talk with Patrick."

Clearly, Jason wasn't pleased as he frowned down at her, but he seemed to understand when he gave her a curt nod. He twirled the diamond on her left finger, lost in thought.

"I'll never be able to give you a diamond like this," he mumbled.

"I never needed a diamond to know you loved me."

"Maybe not, but it suits you. You deserve sparkling diamonds and a big house on a hill. I've only got a log cabin on a mountain."

Liz wondered at his train of thought then came to an abrupt halt when she realized they still hadn't settled the one thing standing in their way. "I can't move back here, Jason."

"What?"

"I thought you would agree to moving."

"My job is here."

"You can find a new job. My life is in Baltimore. I can't risk becoming like my mother," she argued, her heart breaking. Of all the things she needed him to understand, this was number one.

"Would it really be so bad to be like her? She's happy, Lizzie. She's dating; she's got friends. Just because her life isn't what you picture for yourself doesn't mean it's not right. Besides, I like it here." Slowly, his arms slipped from around her waist and he moved away, leaving her cold and alone.

"It doesn't mean it's wrong, either. Is this really going to stand between us again?"

He shrugged. "I want you to see what you've been missing here. I think if you gave it chance instead of running away every time things get tough, you might actually like it here."

"Why can I not be enough for you?"

"I could ask you the same question."

"Stop trying to be rational."

"Someone has to," he shot, his eyes flashing with anger.

"I can't believe you. Patrick is a good man who doesn't deserve to be hurt, but I'm willing to stop my wedding to be with you. Yet, you still refuse to give an inch."

"Something tells me if I give you an inch, you'd take a mile. Isn't it the way it's always been?" Anger pulsed in his jaw.

"No!"

"And if I don't give an inch, you'll go running away, the same way you did before. Anything to avoid giving up what you've envisioned for your life. Have you ever thought maybe you're wrong? Maybe the fancy city life isn't for you, and you might be happier here living the way your mother lives?"

"I hate this town!"

"Hate it so much you'd get married here?"

"I never said the landscape wasn't beautiful," Liz argued, but she knew he made a valid point, and she hated it even more. "My family's here. It was easier this way. You know they can't afford to travel to Baltimore."

"Your family's here, Lizzie. I'm here. You've gotta make a choice."

"I don't know how to choose, Jason. I have a career and friends-a life-in Baltimore. Here, I have..." She trailed off. "How can I just walk away?"

"Everything isn't always going to go your way. You might end up married to Patrick after all. Have two point five kids in the future with a white picket fence around your mansion on a hilltop. But you won't have one thing, Lizzie."

"Oh yeah? What's that?"

"Me."

Chapter 5

The next morning, after a sleepless night full of tears and confusion, Liz walked out of the bedroom and saw Jason sitting on the couch, staring at the frosty windowpane. It appeared as though he'd gotten as much sleep as she did. He nursed a cup of coffee and didn't even acknowledge her presence.

On the table next to him lay a set of keys.

Carefully, he placed the cup of coffee on the end table and turned to face her. "Sooner or later, you're going to have to choose," he said softly. "You can't have us both, and I've never been particularly good at sharing."

"I never said I could have you both."

"I can do it again, though," he continued as if she hadn't spoke, switching his train of thought so fast she couldn't keep up.

"Do what?"

"Let you go."

"I can't do this to Patrick. He loves me, too, Jason, and I don't want to repeat the same mistake I made with you. As much as it hurts to say this, I have to go." During the night, her anger at his inability to budge chaffed her. Combined with the lack of sleep, she felt the hysteria rising in her chest.

"Get dressed. I'm taking you back to town," he ordered.

"What?"

"You heard me," he shot, obviously annoyed. "Get dressed so I can take you back to town. I might not feel so generous in ten minutes."

"Why are you doing this?"

His stone cold gaze narrowed on her. "You've got a wedding to get to."

Silently, he scooped up the keys and tossed them toward her.

"Did you get my car?" But those weren't her keys. "It's to the snowmobile parked outside."

"How did you get one?"

He gave a derisive chuckle, as if he shared a joke with himself.

"It's been here the whole time."

"I had a way to get back to town, and you didn't tell me?"

"Nope."

"How dare you!"

"Forgive me. I was an idiot for believing I might convince you I was the better man. Male pride and all."

"We could have avoided all this if you would have told me the truth! I might have chosen to stay."

Jason smiled distantly. "Sure. Keep telling yourself that."

"Oh, get off your pity pot. You lied to me."

"You never asked. And I didn't volunteer the information."

"It's called lying by omission."

"It's called doing what I thought was best to get you back."

"How did it work out for you, Jason?" She propped her hands on her hips and angled her head.

He smiled and then looked away, back to the windowpane.

"You're not married yet."

Chapter 6

Dressed in white, with a veil tucked neatly in the chignon the local hairdresser had concocted, Liz stared at herself in the mirror. Tilting her head to the side, she eyed the dress more closely. The white satin bodice hugged her curves like a second skin. The capped sleeves cupped her shoulders and extended down her arms with sheer sleeves. A decorative sequined pattern lined the sweetheart neckline. She'd bought it back in Baltimore at a chic bridal boutique. Her friends, Heather and Mary, had come with her to pick it out a few months ago.

Funny how it didn't even come close to representing who she was anymore.

A few days alone with the man who'd haunted her for so many years transformed her back into a country bumpkin. She'd rather wear Jason's flannel shirt and long johns than this ridiculous get up. Or maybe… she wanted to be close to Jason, and wearing his clothes was almost as close as she could get. Almost. She blinked back tears. Why was this happening?

Heather and Mary stood in the corner, whispering to each other. They sensed the change in her. Their suspicious glances confirmed her inability to hide what had happened between her and Jason.

She turned to them and forced a smile, smoothing the front of her dress. "So what do you think of my hometown, girls?"

They exchanged glances. "Liz, are you okay?"

"I'm fine," she insisted with a too-bright smile.

"Have you talked with Patrick? Did he tell you.?" Mary elbowed Heather.

"What happened in that cabin?" Mary asked, taking a step closer, concern written all over her face. "It's like you're going through the motions, but your heart isn't in it anymore."

Liz shrugged. "Jason still loves me." Maybe talking about it with her friends would help her sort out her feelings.

Both of them gave dainty gasps. "Did he say that?" Mary asked.

"Yes."

"What did you say?" Heather grasped Liz's hand and tugged. "The only thing I could say. I still love him, too."

This time both girls remained silent. Heather recovered first. "Look, Liz, I don't think a couple of days in a cabin with your ex constitutes love. Talk to Patrick."

Liz narrowed her eyes and tried not to get her back up. "Patrick doesn't need to know anything. I don't want to hurt him. Jason and I made our choice. There's nothing left for us anymore. Jason's my past, Patrick's my future."

"Why are you going through with the wedding?" Heather asked quietly.

She turned away. It was the very question she'd asked herself all morning. She and Patrick had been dating for over three years. He was perfect spouse material, and she really did love him.

Just not the way she should.

"I don't know," she said honestly. "Patrick understands my need to prove myself through my career. I've never had to justify myself to him. I can be myself."

Her friends seemed at a loss for words. She knew the feeling.

"Maybe we should give you some time alone?" Heather ushered Mary to the door. "We'll be right outside if you need us, but you really need to think this through, Liz. What if you find out Patrick isn't the man you think he is?" The two women hurried through as if running away from her.

Before the words of her bridesmaids registered, the click of the closing door sounded like gunfire, and Liz gave a slight jump. What did that mean? Why wouldn't Patrick be anyone but who she'd always known he was? And why was she so conflicted?

A few days ago, things had been easy. If only she hadn't headed up to the mountain to put Jason behind her, she wouldn't be in this situation. She'd been after some sort of closure, some sort of finality with the situation with Jason. But it hadn't happened.

Instead, she'd been thrown feet first into an avalanche and headfirst back into his life.

Her cell phone rang, bringing her out of her reverie. She didn't recognize the number, but she answered anyway.

"Hello?"

"Still gettin' hitched?" Jason asked on the other end.

"Jason." She hated the way her heart leaped into her throat at the sound of his voice. She couldn't remember one time she'd felt more than companionship with Patrick.

"Are you still getting married, Liz? Answer me."

"Y…yes, Jason. There's nothing left for us. I don't want to live here now, any more than I did then."

"There might be something in your room to change your mind."

Her phone signaled the end of the call and with a grunt of frustration, she put it back on the table.

Looking around the room, she tried to locate anything out of the ordinary. She'd been crammed in this room all day and hadn't noticed anything familiar other than the things she'd brought.

A bouquet of red roses and baby's breath lay on the table next to the door, ready to precede her down the aisle. Her wedding shoes were exactly in front of the fireplace, where she put them earlier. All the figurines on the mantle were unfamiliar.

Moving over to the mantle, she picked up the figurine with wings. It was a typical cupid, holding a bow and arrow. At the end of the arrow was a star instead of a heart. As she turned it over, a frown pulled her lips down. An inscription was handwritten vertically along the angel's legs.

My wish came true, too.

The gentle eyes on the cupid seemed to stare straight through her. Suddenly, the tale Jason told her of the fallen star came to mind. Trailing a finger over Cupid's delicate wings, Liz smiled.

Not even a Valentine's Day wish answered by Cupid himself could keep the doubts away.

Gingerly, she replaced Cupid on the mantle and turned. The table in the corner shone brightly with decorative white lights and tulle. The vision blurred as tears stung her eyelids. A single blink cleared her sight and a tear streaked down her cheek. She swiped at it before it could ruin her makeup.

She studied the table again and saw it.

A faint cry escaped her throat and she ran as quickly as her dress would allow and plucked the miniature off the tabletop.

A tiny, sparkling gazebo decorated in roses had been placed near the back. Her cell phone rang again. She reached over and snatched it up. Before she could say anything, Jason's voice reverberated in her ear.

"I'm going to haunt you forever if you marry him."

Despite her inner turmoil, she couldn't help but grin. "How did you get in here, Jason?"

"I didn't, Cupid did."

Taking a deep breath, Liz gathered her courage to end the ridiculous facade. "Stop calling me. In about five minutes, I'll be walking down the aisle."

"But it'll be me you want standing at the end. Not Patrick. We both know it."

"The cabin was a mistake. I think the concussion was worse than we first believed. It made me act like an idiot."

"You're still acting like an idiot, Lizzie. Now what's your excuse?"

Leave it to Jason to give it to her straight. Had Patrick ever been so honest with her?

"I'm hanging up now," she warned.

"There's one more thing for you, but I suspect you won't find it before you walk down the aisle. Remember one thing for me, okay?" His voice had turned soft, and Liz closed her eyes against the warmth and familiarity of it.

"What's that?"

"I love you. I always have, and I always will."

"Don't ask me to choose, Jason. Please. I love you, but I can't come back here." It would kill her. She'd dry up here. She couldn't be like her mother, unfulfilled and careworn. She had her life. She had her job. And she had Patrick to make it all work, even if she didn't love him the same way she'd always love Jason.

"You'll never love him the same way you love me," he said, reading her mind.

Liz fell silent for a few moments. "You don't know that."

"No, I don't. You left me before because you wanted more than I could give you. Now you're doing it again. All I've ever wanted is you, Lizzie. I've never cared where or how or even why."

It wasn't worth it to start the argument all over again. She hung up the phone without saying goodbye.

Chapter 7

Jason was pretty certain he'd lost Lizzie again. Well, when he was honest with himself, he'd never really had her. The few kisses they'd shared seemed more like a dream now than reality.

Surprisingly, the gifts he'd left behind for her to find hadn't seemed to reach her the way he'd hoped. But there was still one she hadn't seen yet. He'd left that one for last, hidden in her bouquet. If she still married Patrick after seeing it, he'd know for sure whatever they might have had was over; that those passing moments in the cabin with her were folly.

After so many years of living without her, the taste of her still lingered on his lips. How could he sit back and watch her make such a mistake?

Was it a mistake? He'd lived his whole life loving her, and at each turn she'd walked away from him without batting an eyelash. Didn't he deserve more than that?

The answer was a resounding yes, but it didn't change the fact he'd always love Lizzie no matter what. Knowing another man stood at the end of the aisle watching her walking toward him, creating the memory Jason had only envisioned over the years, curled his insides into knots.

He could go to her, stop the wedding and force her to see reason but what guarantee would he have that she wouldn't run again? Fool him once, shame on him, but twice?

A knock at the cabin door sounded, and he knew without answering who it was. His little sister was always there when he needed a friend.

"Hi Shelley," he greeted as he opened the door. She stood there looking so much like his mother he couldn't help but feel another sharp pang of loneliness. He'd missed his parents since they drove to Florida for the winter.

Shelley's dark hair fell around her shoulders and her green eyes bore into him. "Hey. I wanted to make sure you were still here. I was afraid you'd be stupid enough to try and stop Liz's wedding." She stepped around him to move to the couch.

"The thought crossed my mind, but no. It's Lizzie's decision, not mine. I've done all I can." Jason closed the door.

Shelley plumped the throw pillows, a little more vigorously than was necessary. "You're too good for her anyway."

"Shells," he warned, but he was too tired to stop what he knew was coming.

"She walked out on you, Jason. I've watched you mope around for years because you can't be happy without her. You need to put her behind you and move on." Shelley plopped down on the couch and took a sip from his coffee cup.

Cocking his eyebrow, he shook his head. "Seriously, Shelley. I know you're worried about me, but I'll be fine. You can stop the mother hen act."

"I love you, Jason. I want to see you happy. Liz Henley only makes you miserable."

"Not true. I've never been as happy as I am when I'm with her."

Standing, Shelley tossed her hair over her shoulder in habit that had been hers since childhood. "Then it's time to redefine happiness, brother."

When Jason didn't say anything, she shook her head and walked to the door. "Are you sure you're going to make it?"

"Yes. I'll be fine." But Jason didn't trust his own words. He felt like crawling underneath a rock and rolling into the fetal position. Hating how weak and emasculated he suddenly felt, he grabbed the axe laying next to the door. Chopping firewood would help. "Where are you headed all dressed up?" He walked Shelley to the door and opened it for her.

When she didn't answer him, he sighed. "Gotta go with Zeke so he can cover it for the paper, huh?"

"Yeah. I'm sorry, Jason."

"Don't be. I brought it on myself. I should have just left her in the snow."

Shelley gave a derisive snort and hugged him. "Hang in there. I'll check on you afterward."

He didn't need her to define "afterward" to know what she was referring to.

⌒

Liz was brought out of her deep thoughts when the doorknob of the dressing room turned.

Her mother walked through the door and smiled sheepishly. Liz hadn't seen her much since her return to Oakley. Jason was right. Her mother's cheeks were pink, and there was a light in her eyes she'd never noticed during her visits to Baltimore. Liz made a mental note to ask her about it when she returned from her honeymoon.

"Mom? I thought you were in the vestibule, greeting guests." Liz rushed forward and embraced her.

"You look beautiful, honey," she cooed.

Liz studied her. Her dark hair had a few sprinkles of gray in it but was otherwise still the mousey brown Liz had always known it to be. But on her mother, it was stunning. Her brown eyes shined with tears, and her smile trembled.

"Mom, don't cry."

"I can't help it."

"I know you're happy for me, but—"

"No, Liz. You're wrong."

The words stopped Liz short. "What?"

"I know you've always thought I was a nobody here in Oakley."

"What? Mom, did Jason put you up to this?" Her stomach dropped, and her heart thudded. How could her mother have known what she thought about her? And why approach her about it now?

She held her hands up to silence Liz. "Listen to me."

"Okay." Liz sat down on the edge of the couch, and her mother joined her.

"The truth is, Liz, after your father died, I stopped living. I was depressed, and it was hard for me to watch you grow up without your father. You two were always so close."

Liz remembered the lonely years after her father's death, but she'd long since moved past them.

"I never meant for you to think I wasn't happy here, or that my job at the mill wasn't enough. I've made wonderful friends with my co-workers there. That place may be the only job I've ever had and yes, it's tedious work, but it's not as bad as you think it is. Oakley is a wonderful community, and if I could do it all over again, I wouldn't change a thing."

"It's not what I want for my life, Mom."

"Because of me. You only saw my sadness, and you equated that with my job and my life. But in reality, it was because I missed your father."

"I don't understand why you're telling me this now."

"Because I know you were with Jason at the cabin. That boy has loved you since the day you two met. And he's part of the reason I never stopped hoping I'd fall in love again. I saw how much he loved you."

"Mom."

"Don't throw it away because you think you've done better for yourself up north. A career can only go so far. You and Patrick seem happy, but I raised you, Liz. I can see that happiness only goes so deep. Once you're married, that's it. You've made the final choice. I want you to ask yourself one question: Does Patrick make you as happy as Jason does?"

With those final words, her mother kissed her cheek and squeezed her hand before standing.

"Oh, and before I forget, Heather asked me to give you this."

She held out a single sheet of paper.

"Heather?" Heather had just been in here. Why hadn't she said whatever it was on the paper instead of writing it down?

Unfolding the paper and reading the words in Heather's trademark scrawl, Liz frowned.

Patrick came on to me while you were away. He's not who you think he is. And after you told us what happened with Jason, you deserve to know the truth.

Chapter 8

Patrick stood at the end of the aisle as Liz walked toward him.

His smile was wide with happiness.

He was so handsome; one of those men with classic good looks. Sandy blonde hair fell over his brow, and his green eyes watched her with an intensity she'd always appreciated. With him, she was the center of his world.

As she neared, she adjusted her bouquet. She smiled back at her fiancé, ignoring the sick feeling in her gut. Dread was not something she was supposed to be feeling at that particular moment.

The music died down, and the preacher cleared his throat. Before he said anything, Liz reached a finger up and gingerly traced Patrick's jaw. She tried to provoke an emotion, any emotion to tell her she was doing the right thing. Nothing but the same dark emptiness she'd felt since leaving Jason remained.

While she touched him, Patrick's gaze darted over to Heather and Mary. She caught a subtle shake of Mary's head as she made eye contact with him. Heather's eyebrows furrowed, and a frown marred Mary's lips. Looking back to her groom, the truth smacked her with the force of a hurricane. Heather and Mary's warnings. The letter. A lot could happen in the few days she had been away at the cabin with Jason. Had her fiancé made a move on Heather?

Even those revelations didn't come close to the one her mother had given her. Her mother was happy in this little town. Couldn't she be, too?

Patrick's gaze pleaded with her to understand. How could she not? Hadn't she been making out with Jason and told him that she still loved him? Patrick knew even though she'd never really told him about Jason, yet he still stood there, ready to commit. Could she really hold it against him? Yes and no.

The preacher began the ceremony, and Liz looked down at her bouquet. Her life was such a mess.

For years, Heather and Liz had been inseparable. They shopped together, had lunch together, even worked at the same investment firm.

If Heather didn't trust him, should she?

She thought of all the early morning jogs, the comfort of just being together that Patrick offered. Was it possible the comfort stemmed from something Liz once thought impossible? Was Patrick seeing other women for passion, only to come back to her for commitment?

Her gaze focused on something catching the light in the bouquet. Squinting, she raised it a little higher. A small gasp escaped her, and tears welled so fast she had to blink them away to make sure her eyes weren't playing tricks on her.

Nestled against a red rose, just like seven Valentine's Days before, buried beneath the baby's breath with a small, white ribbon in her bouquet was the engagement ring Jason had given her when she was only eighteen. A smile broke out on her face, and she held her hand up to the preacher. He stopped speaking and Liz barely noticed the uneasy shuffle of Patrick's feet in front of her.

Her mother's words echoed in her mind. Jason never once pretended to be something he wasn't. He always challenged her and was so infuriatingly honest with her, it was endearing. After all these years, he still waited for her, still offered his love even though she repeatedly threw it back in his face.

Jason had loved her from the very beginning. He'd never judged her or expected anything from her except love. She'd continually rejected him, yet this one last outreach was her undoing. It didn't matter how long they were separated or how much distance came between them, they were each other's first and only love and nothing would change that.

She thought of his tender ministrations to her wounds in the cabin. The way they'd drunk hot chocolate together in the firelight and how Jason looked at her with all the love she knew he was capable of, causing her heart to lurch. She'd been blinded for so long over her career and leaving Oakley, she hadn't stopped to think about what she really wanted in life.

She wanted Jason. She wanted to fight with him all the time. She didn't want to settle for a life of mediocrity with Patrick. She wanted a life of passion with Jason, and it didn't matter where. If he didn't want to move to Baltimore, she'd come home. Because Oakley was her home. She'd miss the hustle and bustle of city life, but it was a small price to pay to wake up next to Jason and know their love was finally being given a chance.

"Liz?" Patrick's voice penetrated her thoughts.

Looking up into his face, she knew she had to tell him the truth.

"Can I talk to you for a minute?"

Patrick looked around the room. "Now? Here?"

"Let's step outside."

The crowd watched as Patrick and Liz walked down the aisle and exited the building.

"What happened with you and Heather?" she demanded, turning to face him and crossing her arms against the bitter cold.

"You stopped our wedding for this? Do you really think I'd be stupid enough to cheat on you?"

But Liz saw the deceit when he looked away and bit his lip.

"Did you cheat on me or just hit on my best friend?"

With narrowed eyes, Patrick sighed. "Who told you? Heather? Mary? I asked her not to say anything; it was a misunderstanding. Mary didn't hear the whole story."

"I can't marry you, Patrick," she said quickly.

His mouth turned down in a fierce frown. "Yes, you can."

"No, I can't."

Patrick leaned in and mumbled, "Look, she didn't mean anything. She was begging for attention with that red hair and tight shirt."

Heather might be a lot of things, but slut wasn't one of them. "You're talking about my best friend, Patrick. She is a good person. Whatever happened, I'm glad to know that she respected me enough to say no."

Patrick's eyes narrowed. "Does this have anything to do with that ranger you were stranded with?"

"It has everything to do with Jason. I still love him."

"You might want to find out if he still loves you before you go throwing me away."

"Do you really want to be second best?"

"I'll never be second best, sweetheart. But you need to make your choice. It's me or him."

"I choose him. I've chosen him every time, and I didn't realize it."

Patrick shook his head. "Are you serious?"

"Yes." Gently, Liz plucked the engagement ring from her
bouquet and smiled. The small diamond reflected the street lamp-
light.

"You're leaving me for that? That ring couldn't have cost
more than a couple of hundred dollars. I can give you that in
spades."

"A diamond doesn't make me happy. He does."

"How did you get that?" Patrick demanded.

"Jason left it as a little reminder of what's really important."

"And what would that be?"

"Love. You know I've never loved you the way I should have.
You deserve someone who loves you for who you are. If it was a
misunderstanding with Heather, you should apologize. I forgive
you, but she might not."

Patrick looked toward the building then shook his head and
gnashed his teeth. "You're really doing this to me?"

"I'm sorry," Liz whispered. Without another word, she slid
the heavy engagement ring Patrick bought for her off her finger and
handed it to him. In its place, she put Jason's ring where it always
belonged. It still fit her like a glove.

With a final glance at Patrick, she gathered the skirt of her
wedding dress and ran for the horse-drawn carriage down the road,
waiting to take the happy couple to their reception.

A reception that wouldn't happen now.

Chapter 9

Jason ignored the pounding on the front door. He wanted to forget the world existed, especially one important woman who drove him mad. This time, he would get over her. Even faster than before. He'd surround himself with beautiful women and never think about Liz again.

Just thinking that brought to mind Lizzie's curly, brown hair, the hair she'd hated all her life, her silken, chocolate eyes and her luscious curves. Jason knew he couldn't ever meet another woman without comparing the two. And those curls were the perfect length to gather in a fist and kiss her, holding her exactly where he wanted her.

The pounding on the door started up again, and he shook his head. The wedding was over. No doubt it was Shells checking up on him again.

"Go away!" he shouted. He wanted to be alone and be miserable. After everything that had transpired, it was his right.

"Jason, open up!"

His ears were deceiving him, he was sure. That didn't sound like Shelley's voice.

"Jason, it's freezing out here!"

Liz? A grin spread over his face.

So she hadn't gone through with it after all.

He fought down the urge to let out a hoot of jubilation. "Why should I let you in? I should make you suffer the same way you've made me suffer!"

"I'm seriously freezing my tail off out here. Please open up."

He thought he heard her teeth chattering through the door. He refused to acknowledge the tug of sympathy in his chest.

"I don't have anything to say to a married woman."

"I didn't do it, Jason, and you know it."

"I don't know anything except you left me high and dry again."

"If you open the door, I promise you, I'll never leave. Again."

He couldn't help the fool smile on his face. "That could get annoying. And I seem to have heard those words before."

"I mean it this time!"

"Heard that one, too."

"Jason!"

He covered his mouth to hide the chuckle. "A man doesn't like having his pride stepped all over, Lizzie," he said as seriously as he could.

"You'll get over it. Now open up."

After a few moments of silence, she pounded again, "I know you're punishing me. But Patrick is still at the church. It might not be too late to tell him I changed my mind."

"I told you he was an idiot."

"You're the idiot, Kenyon! Open this door!"

He unlocked the door and swung it open in one swoop. He blocked her entrance with his body. She stood there, blending in with the white, snowy background in her wedding dress. He'd never seen her look so beautiful.

Soft brown curls framed her face, and the veil at her nape blew in the wind. Her brown eyes searched his until she finally held up her ring finger.

His engagement ring was there.

"I found your last gift."

"Happy Valentine's Day. I never wanted to see it again."

Angling her head, her lips curved upward. "Unless it was on my finger?"

"No, not even then."

She frowned. "I thought you still loved me."

"Lizzie, I can't take much more of your indecision. Either you want me or you don't. It's that simple."

"I'm standing here, aren't I? In the cold in a wedding dress?" she added a little desperately.

"Yes, you are. But the very fact you're in that wedding dress tells me you're still not one hundred percent sure."

"Oh, good grief!" She pushed him inside and went straight to the fire, holding her hands out toward the licking flames.

"How far did you make it? Did you stop it before you walked down the aisle or did you make it all the way to your fiancé before you dropped the news you couldn't marry him?"

She shot him a wry glance over her shoulder. "The preacher had already begun."

"Wow." He couldn't help but grin. "So, tell me again why you're here?"

Dropping her hands against her thighs with a thwack, she frowned. "Are you going to make me spell it out?"

"Of course."

"I had a talk with my mother. She made me think about some things. And I love you. Now are you going to take me back or not?"

He loved her spunk. "Not."

Her wide, chocolate eyes rounded in surprise. "Are you serious?"

The shock on her face was too much for him. Throwing his head back in laughter, there wasn't any reason to keep up the charade except to see her squirm. But he couldn't stand not taking her in his arms any longer.

Sobering, he walked forward and took her hand in his. "No, I'm not serious. In fact, I'm not letting you go ever again. I'll duct tape you to a chair if I have to."

"Sounds kinky." She angled him a catty, raised eyebrow and grinned.

"I love you, too, Lizzie. It's time for us to be together, don't you think?"

"I know it is. I'll settle everything back in Baltimore and move back here with you. I think I'd like to come home for a little while, see if Oakley has changed any."

"Are you sure? Oakley hasn't changed one bit. I mean, I'm not moving, so it's going to have to be you," he said with a smile.

She smacked his arm with her palm. "I'll move. If it means being here with you."

"This won't be easy. I'm guessing we're going to fight more than we get along."

"It's what we do. I wouldn't expect anything less." She stepped into his arms and hooked her fingers behind his neck.

Unable to help himself, he wrapped his arms around her waist and snatched her close. "Lizzie, I need to know you're not going to run again when things get tough."

"I thought we'd covered that already." Her eyes bore into his. "What if you move back here and decide you're not happy?

What if we get to know each other all over again, and we're not the same as we used to be? Are you going to leave me again?"

"Nope. I'm not worried about any of that."

Her voice was so certain Jason did a double take.

"I'm not," she insisted. "Every day since I walked away from you has led me back here. I haven't been able to fall in love, and I've been searching for something this whole time. It wasn't until I looked down and saw the ring in my bouquet that I realized what it was."

Jason waited. He needed to hear her say it.

"You," she whispered, tears glistening in her eyes.

Lowering his lips to hers, he claimed her mouth. Tightening his hold, Jason gave her a kiss meant to weaken her knees and cause her to submit. With a soft sigh, he knew the moment he accomplished his goal. Her body lay against his, and she angled her head.

He pulled away, denying her what she wanted most. Her eyes opened then narrowed at him. "What now?"

"Marry me." This was the last step. If she was serious about being with him, marrying him was the only way.

"I'm wearing your ring, aren't I?"

"It's a piece of jewelry, Lizzie."

She moved away from him then, back to the fire. Staring into the flickering flames, he wasn't sure what she would say next. Twirling the ring around on her finger, she studied it.

When her gaze rose to meet his, her tears streamed down her cheeks and broke his heart. He should have known.

"Yes," she whispered. "I'll marry you."

"Come again?" He tilted his ear toward her to make sure his heart wasn't in his throat for no reason.

"I'll marry you, Jason. Let's elope. Go to Vegas or something."

He was afraid he was hearing things. "There's no way I'm going to elope with you when I've waited so long to show you off." She smiled. "I can't marry you today, though. Today was my day with Patrick. Can we wait a few days? I don't want to think about him when I marry you."

Jason stepped forward and touched her jaw. "What about midnight on New Year's Eve? A new year, a new beginning, just for us."

Lizzie's eyes lit brightly. "That sounds perfect, Jason. Absolutely perfect. Now come on, there's a horse and carriage waiting to give us a ride around town. I have it for the next hour."

"Horse and carriage?"

Lizzie grinned, and tugged his arm. "Complete with roses and lights. I want you all to myself for a little while. And the deposit was non-refundable." She sighed at his grin. "I love you."

"Promise?"

"With all my heart."

Chapter 10

The steady clomp of the horses' hooves slowed as they neared the Oakley Chamber of Commerce on the outskirts of town. The people were at what would have been her reception with Patrick, and the party was in full swing. Liz smiled. She'd never been happier that she hadn't gone through with something.

"Where do you think Patrick went off to?" Jason asked next to her as they rode by the reception. The carriage did a u-turn and headed back to the middle of the town. With a blanket thrown over their lap and Jason's arms around Liz's shoulders, the night couldn't have been more perfect.

"I don't care. Have you looked at the sky tonight? The stars seem so much brighter than usual."

Jason squeezed her close. "Love has a nice way of opening your eyes."

Liz couldn't help but giggle. "You know everyone is going to be really happy for us."

"Ecstatic."

Liz took in her surroundings. The cold nip to the air faded when she leaned her head against Jason's shoulder, and he pulled her close. The carriage passed the double doors of the Chamber of Commerce again, and the few milling about outside nodded a greeting at their passing.

The trees were still heavy-laden with snow, and the drifts against the side of the building rose to the bottom of the windowsill at on the west side of the building. She could see the side of the gazebo behind the building lit romantically with white lights and roses, the way it had been decorated when Jason first proposed to her.

They were silent until the carriage rounded the square at the oak tree the town was built around. Jason signaled for the driver to stop.

He turned to Liz. "Will you dance with me? Right here in the middle of town for everyone to see?" Jason maneuvered out of the carriage and offered Liz his hand.

"My lady," he said with a dramatic flair.

When she was stepping from the carriage, at the last second, he grabbed her around the waist and twirled her to the ground.

As they walked to the square together, soft music floated over the town's speaker system and a few onlookers stared from across the street. Liz and Jason walked into the square. Everyone else slid into the shadows as Jason pulled her into his arms.

"I could get used to this." Liz sighed.

"Good. It's about time we get used to being together. So what was the deciding factor? It had to be more than the ring." He dropped light kisses along her jaw in between his sentences.

"Talking to my mom. She opened my eyes to some things I never saw before. I'll have to tell you about it sometime."

"I'd like that."

"And when you took me back to town, Patrick met me there. I noticed he had a cut on his lip. He said he broke up a fight at Beaver's, so I didn't think much about it."

"What happened?"

"Heather sent a note with my mom. It seemed like the world was trying to tell me something. The split on Patrick's lip was from him making a move on Heather. She decided to make a move on him."

Jason's gaze settled on hers, and he smiled at her. It was the loving smile he used to give her so long ago. "So this is really happening, huh?"

"It appears so," she said, licking her lips. Liz pinched the soft skin on the underside of his arm.

"Ow! What was that for?"

"Just making sure I'm not dreaming."

"It doesn't work that way. You're supposed to pinch yourself or let me pinch you."

Liz batted her lashes. "But it's so much more fun the way I did it."

He narrowed playful eyes on her. "If I didn't love you so much, I'd turn you over my knee right now."

Liz winked. "Maybe later."

As the song ended, Jason pulled her close and covered her mouth with his. She loved the softness in which he handled her that contradicted his rock hard body. His kiss was one of exploration and new beginnings.

Gently, he pulled away. His hold around her waist tightened and he pressed his cheek against hers. It forced them both to look at the white, twinkling gazebo lights, as well as from every light post in town.

"Happy Valentine's Day, Jason."

"This is the best one yet," Jason said. "Happy Valentine's Day, Lizzie."

About the Author

Stephanie Taylor is a homeschooling mom of three by day and a writer and business owner by night. She has a doctorate in Multitasking and can actually walk a tight rope while preparing dinner with one hand and typing her next novel with the other. You can find her online on Facebook and Twitter or at her publishing company, Clean Reads.

Stephanie loves to hear from her readers!

Twitter: @cleanreads
Facebook: stephanietaylorastraeapress
www.cleanreads.com
staylorauthor@gmail.com